HIT THE BASKET

BY JONNY ZUCKER
ILLUSTRATED BY PETE SMITH

Titles in the FULL FLIGHT runway series

Level 3
Goal!	Jane A C West
Too Hot	Roger Hurn/Alison Hawes

Level 4
A Big Catch	Alison Hawes
Deyda's Drum	Roger Hurn
The Strawberry Thief	Alison Hawes
Billy's Boy	Melanie Joyce

Level 5
Cage Boy	Jillian Powell
Master Blasters	Melanie Joyce
Game Player King	Stan Cullimore
In the Zone	Tony Norman

Level 6
Dodgems	Jane A C West
Tansy Smith	Helen Orme

Level 7
Pirate Attack	Jonny Zucker
Hitting the Basket	Jonny Zucker

Badger Publishing Limited
Oldmedow Road,
Hardwick Industrial Estate,
King's Lynn PE30 4JJ
Telephone: 01438 791037
www.badgerlearning.co.uk
2 4 6 8 10 9 7 5 3

Hitting the Basket ISBN 978 1 84691 857 5

Publisher: David Jamieson
Editor: Danny Pearson
Design: Fiona Grant
Illustration: Pete Smith

HITTING THE BASKET

CONTENTS

Vocabulary
Basketball
Excited
Practice
Embarrassed
Shocked
Defending

Main characters

Atash and Gulnar

CHAPTER 1
BASKET STARS

Atash and Gulnar were outside their flat. They were playing basketball.

They were throwing a basketball to each other.

Atash threw the ball to Gulnar. Gulnar caught it.

She aimed with her left hand and threw the ball.

It flew in the air and she scored a basket.

Atash and Gulnar were from Afghanistan. They had been in Britain a short time.

They were both very good at basketball.

They were the best basketball players at Greenwood school.

They had become the school team's basketball stars!

Since they had arrived at Greenwood, the basketball team had done very well.

"Well done for reaching the basketball cup final," said their coach, Mr Reed.

Atash and Gulnar were both very excited about reaching the final.

"But the final will be hard," said Mr Reed. "You will be playing Mayland School."

Atash and Gulnar had been told about Mayland.

Mayland were a very good team. Mayland were a fantastic team!

"We will lose the final," said one of the Greenwood players.

"No," said Atash. "We have a chance."

Over the next few days, the Greenwood team worked hard.

Atash and Gulnar worked extra hard.

They practised their passing.
They practised their shooting.
They practised their defending.

Then the day of the final came.

CHAPTER 2
THE FINAL

Atash and Gulnar were very nervous.
So were the other Greenwood players.

They got changed. They ran onto
the basketball court to practise.

They practised their passing.
They practised their shooting.
Then the Mayland team walked out.

They were much bigger than the Greenwood
players.

"How come they are so big?" asked Atash in
surprise.

The match started and Greenwood played
well.

Atash and Gulnar both played well.

They both had lots of shots.
They both scored good baskets.

But the Mayland players were tall and fast.
They were much taller and much faster than
the Greenwood players.

Mayland scored basket after basket.

Atash and Gulnar played their best.
They ran and they passed and they shot.
But it was no good. Mayland scored more
baskets than Greenwood.

Mayland won the game.

They went up to collect the trophy.

In the changing room everyone from
Greenwood was quiet.

They had not won the match.
They'd lost the match.

They started to leave the changing room.

CHAPTER 3
THAT'S UNFAIR

Atash and Gulnar did not talk.

They were very upset about losing the final.
They took a wrong turn and ended up in a
corridor.

They were outside a room with an open door.
They went into the room.

Atash saw a piece of paper on the table.
He read the piece of paper and was shocked.

"Look at this!" he said.

"What is it?" asked Gulnar.

"It's about the Mayland team," said Atash. "It shows how old they are."

"How old are they?" asked Gulnar.

"They are all one year older than us," said Atash. "That is why they are so big."

"But that's unfair!" cried Gulnar. "If they are one year older than us, then they cheated."

"You are right!" shouted Atash, "Come on Gulnar, let's go!"

13

They ran back down the corridor and found the referee.

They showed him the piece of paper. He took a long look at it.

"The Mayland players are a year older than us," said Gulnar.

"That's not fair!" said the referee. "You should all be the same age!"

Atash and Gulnar nodded.

"What are you going to do?" asked Gulnar.

"I am going to sort this out," said the referee.

The referee called both teams back.

"The Mayland players are a year older than the Greenwood players," he said.

The Mayland players and their coach looked very embarrassed.

"So the trophy now goes to Greenwood!" said the referee.

Atash and Gulnar were very, very happy.

"Go up and collect the trophy," Mr. Reed told them.

They went up to collect the trophy.
"It was lucky we got lost!" laughed Atash.

Where are Atash and Gulnar from?

Atash and Gulnar play for the Greenwood School team, who are they playing against?

What three things do Atash and Gulnar practise the most?

How did the Mayland team cheat?

Who went up to collect the trophy?

Water Life

Contents

17

Vocabulary

Useful
Angrily
Equipment
Smashed
Everyone
Cheered

Main characters

Salima

Salima's Mum

Two water engineers

Chapter 1
Thirsty

Salima loved riding her bike.

She could ride fast. She could ride slow.
She could do bike tricks.

"Why do you always ride that bike?" said her
Mum.

"Why don't you do something useful?"

In Salima's village there was no water.
So every day Salima had to walk.

She had to walk to get water.

It was five miles to the old water pump.
And five miles back.
Salima walked to the pump with her Mum.

The walk was very long. The walk was very hot.

It was very tiring.

"I hate this walk," said Salima.
"I just want to ride my bike."

"Forget about that bike!" said her Mum.

Chapter 2
Visitors

One morning a man and a woman arrived.

They came with a team of people.
They came with a lot of equipment.

"Why are you here?" Salima asked.

"We want your village to have water," said the man.

The man, the woman and their team worked hard all day.

They dug a very deep hole.

Salima was on her bike. "Have you found water yet?" she asked.

"Not yet," said the woman.

Salima wanted them to find water now.

It was getting dark when Salima heard a shout.

There below - a long way down - was water.

"YES!" shouted Salima.

"Can we get the water out now?" asked Salima.

"We need to fit a pump," said the woman. "The pump will bring water up and out."

"How long will that take?" asked Salima crossly.

"Our team will work through the night," said the man.

"The pump will be ready in the morning," said the woman.

Salima woke up early the next day.

The man and the woman were by the hole.
They looked unhappy.

Big metal poles were coming out of the hole.

"These metal poles need to be pushed round
for the pump to work," said the man.

Salima pushed one. It did not move.

"We do not have enough power to make the
pump work," said the man.

"Didn't you know about this before you came?" asked Salima angrily.

"We did not know the water would be such a long way down," said the woman.

"That makes it very hard for the pump to work," said the man.

"Couldn't we all push it?" asked Salima.

"The whole village would have to push all day, every day for it to give just a tiny bit of water," said the woman.

Salima was very upset.

Chapter 3
Pedal Power

That day Salima and her Mum walked to the old water pump. Five miles there and five miles back.

Salima was hot and cross. I wish the pump worked, she thought.

When they got back she rode her bike round and round the hole.

"Stop riding that bike!" shouted her Mum. "And do something useful!"

Suddenly Salima had an idea. She sped over
to the man and woman.

She told them her idea. "What a clever idea,"
said the man.

That night the man and woman left the
village.

Three days later they came back.
They came with lots more equipment.

They and their team worked hard all day.

As it was getting dark, they finished.

"Salima get all of your friends!" shouted the woman.

Round the hole were lots of seats and bike pedals.

"Everyone sit down and pedal!" shouted Salima.

Everyone started pedalling. But nothing happened.

"FASTER!" shouted Salima.

Everyone pedalled faster.

Suddenly, a few drops of water dripped out of the pipe.

A minute later, water started flowing out.

"YOU HAVE DONE IT SALIMA!" shouted the woman.

Salima and her friends pedalled.
The water kept gushing out.

"You have done something very good!"
said the woman.

"I do not know what gave her the idea!"
said Salima's Mum.

"You said do something useful!" grinned
Salima.

Questions

Where does Salima live?

How far away was the old pump?

When did the man and women tell Salima the new pump would be ready for?

Who gave Salima the idea of using pedal power for the new pump?

Where do you get your drinking water from?

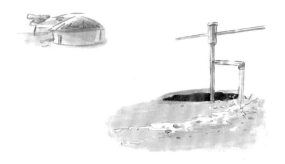